PUFFIN BOOKS

SHADOWS OF MAGIC

Linda Chapman lives in Leicestershire with her
family and two Bernese mountain dogs. When
she is not writing she spends her time looking
after her two young daughters, horse riding and
teaching drama.

Books by Linda Chapman

BRIGHT LIGHTS

CENTRE STAGE

NOT QUITE A MERMAID series

MY SECRET UNICORN series

STARDUST series

Stardust

SHADOWS OF MAGIC

Linda Chapman
Illustrated by Angie Thompson

PUFFIN

PUFFIN BOOKS

Published by the Penguin Group
Penguin Books Ltd, 80 Strand, London WC2R ORL, England
Penguin Group (USA) Inc., 375 Hudson Street, New York, New York 10014, USA
Penguin Group (Canada), 90 Eglinton Avenue East, Suite 700, Toronto, Ontario, Canada M4P 2Y3
(a division of Pearson Penguin Canada Inc.)
Penguin Ireland, 25 St Stephen's Green, Dublin 2, Ireland (a division of Penguin Books Ltd)
Penguin Group (Australia), 250 Camberwell Road, Camberwell, Victoria 3124, Australia
(a division of Pearson Australia Group Pty Ltd)
Penguin Books India Pvt Ltd, 11 Community Centre, Panchsheel Park, New Delhi – 110 017, India
Penguin Group (NZ), 67 Apollo Drive, Rosedale, North Shore 0632, New Zealand
(a division of Pearson New Zealand Ltd)
Penguin Books (South Africa) (Pty) Ltd, 24 Sturdee Avenue, Rosebank, Johannesburg 2196,
South Africa

Penguin Books Ltd, Registered Offices: 80 Strand, London WC2R ORL, England

penguin.com

Published 2007
2

Set in Monotype Bembo
Typeset by Palimpsest Book Production Limited
Grangemouth, Stirlingshire

Made and printed in England by Clays Ltd, St Ives plc

British Library Cataloguing in Publication Data
A CIP catalogue record for this book is available from the British Library

ISBN: 978-0-141-32208-7

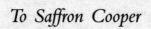

To Saffron Cooper

CHAPTER

One

'Bye, Lucy,' Mr Evans said as he heaved Lucy's suitcase into the boot of the car.

Mrs Evans smoothed Lucy's long, chestnut hair. 'Have a lovely holiday.'

'Bye!' Lucy gave her mum and dad a massive hug.

'We'll ring you when we get to Wales,' Xanthe Greenwood promised. Xanthe and her daughter Allegra lived next door to Lucy's family and the two girls were best friends.

Mrs Evans glanced up at the clear blue April sky. 'It should be lovely in Pembrokeshire if the weather stays like this.'

'We don't care, even if it rains,' Allegra said. 'We're going to have fun, aren't we, Lucy?'

The two girls grinned at each other. They always had fun together. Not just in the day like normal ten-year-olds, but at night too. This was because they were stardust spirits.

Everyone is made out of stardust, Allegra had told Lucy when they had first met just over a year ago, *but some people have more stardust than others.*

She had gone on to tell Lucy that if

these people believed in magic enough, they could turn themselves into stardust spirits at night-time. Stardust spirits looked after nature, putting right any wrongs done by thoughtless humans. To help them do this, they could fly and do magic. There were four types of stardust spirit – summer, autumn, winter and spring – and each type could do different magic. Lucy was a summer spirit, which meant she could start fires and cast protective shields.

Lucy loved going to the woods at night with all her stardust friends. And now she was really looking forward to her holiday. Xanthe was also a stardust spirit and her friends who they were going to stay with in Wales – Fran and David and their daughter Tess – were all stardust spirits as well.

Lucy hugged herself happily as she got into the car. A whole week of being surrounded by other stardust spirits and of being by the seaside. It sounded like the best holiday ever!

Xanthe started the engine. Lucy waved out of the back window at her mum and dad until they turned out of the driveway and she couldn't see them anymore.

'This is going to be great!' Allegra said happily as she settled back into her seat.

'It is,' Xanthe agreed, turning the radio on. 'Pembrokeshire's a very beautiful place. There's so much wildlife there – dolphins and seals in the water, sea birds like puffins and kittiwakes and, in the hills, ponies and deer. It's also one of the most magical places in Britain. You'll find it easy to do magic there, Lucy. But you must be careful.'

'Why?' Lucy asked curiously.

'Well, you know that you have a lot

of stardust inside you?' Xanthe said.

Lucy nodded. She knew she could do all sorts of magic that ten-year-old stardust spirits couldn't normally to do. No one seemed to know why she was so powerful. Lucy didn't really care. She just liked being able to do lots of magic!

'I've noticed that it's not just the stardust inside you that makes you so powerful,' Xanthe told her. 'You also seem to have the unusual ability to attract stardust from the skies.'

Lucy had drawn on the magic in the skies and used it to help her do magic many times. She hadn't realized that doing this was unusual though.

'Can't other people do it?' she asked in surprise.

'Most stardust spirits can learn how to do it, but you're like a natural channel. Stardust just seems to be attracted to you. It wants to flow into you.'

'This is so not fair,' Allegra complained to Lucy. 'Not only have you got lots of stardust inside you but you attract more of it! I wish I could do as much magic as you!'

'You have power enough of your own,' Xanthe told her. 'You're a very strong spirit for your age. Don't compare yourself to Lucy, Allegra.'

'Why?' Allegra said.

Xanthe raised her eyebrows. 'Just because.'

Allegra sighed. 'I hate it when you say that.'

'Tough,' Xanthe said, with a teasing smile. 'Look, Lucy, this isn't something you really need to worry about,' she said reassuringly. 'I just want you to be careful. In an area where there is a lot of magic you may find that even more power flows into you. If your magic gets stronger it'll be tempting to draw even more down from the skies. But you must remember that as stardust spirits we should only use the power we need and not seek power for its own sake.'

Lucy nodded. She'd learnt that lesson before when they'd been dealing with a dark spirit the summer before. Dark spirits were stardust spirits who had turned bad because they loved power so much they would do anything to get it – including taking it from other stardust spirits. She had no intention of ever becoming one of them. 'I'll be careful,' she promised.

As she spoke a report came on the radio about a mini tornado that had hit a village in Dorset the day before. 'Hang on,' Xanthe said, turning the radio up. 'I want to listen to this.'

'The tornado travelled for eight kilometres,' the radio presenter was saying, 'and reached wind speeds of up to one hundred and fifty kilometres per hour. Witnesses described it as a swirling vortex that struck the village. Luckily no one was seriously injured.'

Xanthe looked worried.

'What is it, Xanthe?' Allegra asked. She always called Xanthe by her real

name, never 'Mum'. At first it had
seemed strange to Lucy but not any
more. Xanthe was young for a mum
and sometimes she seemed more like
Allegra's older sister. Neither Xanthe
nor Allegra ever saw Allegra's dad.

'Something's not right,' replied
Xanthe. 'There's been a number of
strange things happening with the
weather recently – flash floods last
month, now this tornado and a few
weeks ago there was a mini
earthquake. To get such a combination
of things happening suggests that
there's an imbalance in nature; that
something is interfering with the
stardust in the sky.'

'Could it be a dark spirit?' Allegra
asked, her blue eyes wide.

'A normal dark spirit couldn't cause so many problems,' Xanthe replied.

'So there might be lots of them working together?' Lucy said in alarm.

'I don't know.' Xanthe glanced over her shoulder. 'It isn't something either of you need to worry about though.'

'But —' Allegra began.

'I'm not discussing it any more,' Xanthe said firmly and she turned the radio up.

Lucy glanced at Allegra. Dark spirits! She couldn't wait till she and Allegra were alone so they could talk about it.

Xanthe drove on in silence. It was clear she was thinking about something. They crossed into Wales and drove along the south coast. At

times they could see the blue-grey sea
racing into sandy coves. The cliffs
were sheer and seagulls circled
overhead. Small islands were dotted
out at sea. The sun was just starting to
set in the sky.

'We're almost there now,' Xanthe
looked at Lucy. 'I've been thinking –
while we're away, Lucy, it might be
best if you keep the full extent of
your powers secret. I've told Fran,
David and Tess – the friends who
we'll be staying with – how powerful
you are but I don't think the other
stardust spirits there need to know. Be
careful about showing your full
powers, OK?'

'OK,' Lucy agreed in surprise. 'But
why?'

Xanthe sighed and opened her mouth, but before she could speak, Allegra chipped in. 'Just because,' she said with a grin.

Xanthe's eyes twinkled. 'You said it, Allegra!'

She drove into a small town. There was a seafront with shops selling holiday things like inflatable toys and beach towels, an ice-cream parlour and a fish and chip shop. There was a wide promenade and down on the beach Lucy could see people walking their dogs on the golden sands, and children climbing on the rocks at the foot of the steep cliffs.

Fran and David's house was on a road just back from the seafront. It was a big old house in a row of other houses.

Xanthe parked on the driveway. Before
they had even got out of the car the
house's front door was thrown open and
a man and a woman came out. The
woman was very pretty with short dark
hair and deep-brown eyes. The man had
his hair tied back in a ponytail.

'Fran! David!' Xanthe said, getting
out of the car.

They came forward and greeted her
and Allegra. Lucy hung back feeling
shy but the next minute Fran was
giving her a warm hug. 'You must be
Lucy. It's lovely to meet you. I hope
you'll have a great time here.'

Lucy's shyness melted away. 'Thanks!'
she said, smiling.

Fran turned. 'Tess!' she called.
'Everyone's here!'

A girl just a bit older than Lucy and Allegra came out of the house. She stopped on the doorstep. She had long dark hair and brown eyes just like Fran's. She gave Lucy a quick, cool look and then turned to Allegra. 'Hi,' she said, smiling.

'Hi, Tess,' Allegra replied. 'This is Lucy.'

Tess glanced at Lucy but didn't say

anything. Lucy frowned. Was she imagining it or was Tess being deliberately unfriendly?

'I'm sure you three are going to get on just great,' David said. 'Tess, why don't you show Allegra and Lucy where their room is?'

Tess turned to Allegra. 'It's this way.' Allegra and Lucy followed her into the house.

As they walked up the stairs, Tess chatted to Allegra. 'It's ages since I saw you. Mum said you moved last year. So where does your stardust group meet at night?'

'In the woods near our village in Devon,' Allegra replied. 'It's a really ancient woodland.'

'How about you? Where does your

stardust group meet?' Lucy asked Tess.

Tess looked as if it was a really dumb question. 'On the beach, of course.' She turned pointedly to Allegra. 'So what sort of animals have you been looking after in your woods?'

While Allegra started telling Tess about the otters, honey buzzards and dormice, Lucy stared at the older girl's back. She was being really unfriendly.

They reached the top of the third staircase. 'This is your room,' Tess said.

It was a large bedroom with a wooden floor and two beds covered in soft patchwork quilts, and a big sash window that opened on to the garden. It was getting dark outside. Lucy went to the window. 'What type of stardust spirit are you?' she asked Tess.

'Summer,' Tess replied.

'Like me,' Lucy said.

'I know,' Tess answered, and Lucy had the distinct feeling that she wasn't that pleased about it.

Just then David came into the room with their cases.

'Here you go, girls. Why don't you unpack, we'll have some supper and then we can go and meet the other stardust spirits on the beach. That sound OK?'

'Definitely!' Allegra replied. Lucy smiled and nodded. Even if Tess was making her feel unwelcome, Fran and David certainly weren't.

'Come on, Tess,' David said. 'Leave Allegra and Lucy to unpack.'

As soon as they had gone, Lucy

turned to Allegra. 'I thought you said Tess was nice!'

'She is usually,' Allegra said.

'Well, she's acting like she wishes I wasn't here,' Lucy muttered.

'Don't worry about it,' Allegra said. 'I bet she'll be fine later.' She sat down on one of the beds and looked at Lucy eagerly. 'So what do you think about all that stuff Xanthe was talking about in the car? Do you think there are some dark spirits causing problems?'

'There's certainly been loads of weird things happening with the floods and stuff,' Lucy said. 'If it is dark spirits, I wonder where they are.'

'Maybe near here,' Allegra said.

Lucy shivered. 'I hope not.' She vividly remembered the horrible dizzy feeling she had experienced every time she was near to Maggie, the dark spirit they had come across in the summer. It was the effect that dark spirits had on normal stardust spirits.

Xanthe called up the stairs. 'Girls! Supper's ready!'

'Coming!' Allegra shouted. 'The sooner we have supper, the sooner we can turn into stardust spirits!' she said to Lucy.

Lucy jumped off the bed and together they ran down the stairs.

CHAPTER
TWO

'I believe in stardust,' Lucy and Allegra said together. It was after supper and they were standing side by side in front of their open bedroom window. 'I believe in stardust. *I believe in stardust!*'

As they said the words for the third time, Lucy felt a rushing, dissolving sensation as if all the weight was dropping away from her body. She

twirled up into the air, her jeans
turning into a golden dress that
shimmered like morning sunbeams.

Allegra flew out through the
window, her blonde curls bouncing on
her shoulders. 'Come on!' she
exclaimed, her silver dress glittering in
the starlight. Each type of stardust spirit
wore different colour clothes. Summer
spirits wore gold, autumn spirits wore
silver, spring spirits wore green and
winter spirits wore blue.

As they flew into the night sky, they
saw Xanthe waiting for them. Fran,
David and Tess had gone on ahead to
the meeting place but Xanthe had
insisted that the girls unpacked first.

'Ready?' she asked as they flew
down to join her.

'Ready!' Lucy and Allegra chorused.

'Then let's go!' Xanthe flew into the air and seemed to disappear.

Lucy and Allegra followed her, camouflaging themselves against the starry sky in case anyone saw them. All stardust spirits could use magic to camouflage themselves – to blend into the background. It made it look as though they had vanished but if you knew what to look for you could see a faint outline in the air.

Xanthe led the way across the town towards cliff tops where the short grass grew alongside mounds of pink heather and prickly gorse bushes. At the bottom of the steep grey cliffs the sea pulled at the sand.

'Fran and David's group meet in a

secret cove not far from here,' Xanthe said, letting her camouflage drop now they were safely out of the town. 'They look after all the wildlife of the beach, the sea and the cliff tops. While we are here you'll be expected to help out with tasks, just like you do in the woods at home.'

'Cool!' Allegra said. 'Maybe we'll get to look after seals or dolphins.'

Xanthe swooped over the cliff edge, towards the sea. They followed her. A large sandy cove was spread out in front of them. It curved round in a semi-circle, the edges on each side bordering on to jagged rocks that would be impassable without a boat. The sea lapped against the sand and all around the cove were lots of stardust spirits. Some were flying in the air, others were standing on the sand talking. A gang of teenage stardust spirits were sitting on a ledge of rock halfway up the cliff.

As Xanthe, Allegra and Lucy flew into the cove, lots of the stardust spirits called out to Xanthe and flew over.

Xanthe hugged and kissed her friends. 'Hi, everyone! It's lovely to see you. This is Allegra, my daughter – and her friend Lucy Evans.'

'I remember you from the last time you visited,' a woman with red hair and a blue dress said with a smile to Allegra. 'It's great to see you again. My name's Bethan. I hope you have fun while you're staying here.'

'Have you heard about the tornado?' a male stardust spirit asked Xanthe. 'What do you think is happening?'

'I don't know, Mark. It is worrying,' Xanthe said seriously. She paused and quickly glanced round to where Allegra and Lucy were listening. 'Why don't you two go and find Fran?'

'She's down by the rock pools telling the younger ones what she'd like them to do tonight,' Bethan said. 'I'll take you over there.'

Rather reluctantly, Lucy and Allegra followed her. 'I wanted to stay and hear what your mum was going to say,' Lucy whispered to Allegra.

'Me too,' Allegra whispered back. 'It sounds like people here are worried about stuff too.'

Fran smiled as they flew over. 'Hi, girls. Everyone, this is Allegra and Lucy. They're staying for the week.'

There were ten stardust spirits around her. They smiled and began to say their names. Tess was standing with two girls, one with thick shoulder-length blonde hair cut into layers, and another with waist-length brown hair. The blonde girl was called Lottie and the girl with brown hair was called Bea.

'We were just talking about the things that need doing tonight,' Fran went on after everyone had introduced themselves. 'Maybe you two could help with the polecats.'

'Polecats?' Lucy said, intrigued. 'What are they?'

'You haven't heard of polecats?' Tess
snorted.

Fran shot her a surprised look.
'Don't be like that, Tess. They don't
have polecats where Lucy is a stardust
spirit. Polecats are a bit like large
ferrets,' she explained to Lucy. 'They're
a protected species. At the moment
there are some living in an old rabbit
warren in the cliffs above the next
cove along from here. I'd like to find
out how many there are but it's hard
because they spend a lot of their time
underground. I thought by watching
tonight we might get an idea. Will you
help with that?'

'Of course,' Lucy said, very grateful
that Fran hadn't made her feel stupid
and small.

Fran gave everyone jobs to do. Some people were going to check on some seals that were living close by; others were going to check on the birds on the heathland. 'Come back here when the star of Aldebaran sets and we can see how everyone has got on,' Fran said.

Lucy and Allegra flew round to the next bay. It was covered in short grass and heather with rocky outcropping. There were lots of rabbit holes and Allegra and Lucy sat down to wait. Ten minutes later they were rewarded by a black nose and whiskery white muzzle sticking out of a hole. The whiskers twitched and then a head popped out.

'It's a polecat!' Allegra hissed.

Lucy stared at the creature. It had

triangular-shaped pointed ears and lively dark eyes that darted around. It bounded out of the hole on its short stubby legs. It moved a bit like an otter. Seeing the girls, it stopped and froze. Lucy held out her hand. 'Hey there,' she murmured.

The polecat looked at her warily. Lucy kept very still. Most animals were happy to come to stardust spirits. To her delight, the polecat bounded towards her. It sniffed her hand and then put its front paws on her knee and stared into her face.

'You're beautiful!' Lucy said, very gently stroking its fur.

'I bet this is its mate,' Allegra whispered as a second polecat popped its head out of the hole. 'Oh, wow!

Look at her tummy!' she gasped. 'She
looks pregnant.'

Lucy looked at the second polecat.
She was smaller than the first apart
from her very round belly.

The two polecats scampered around
the cliff top for a few minutes then
disappeared back into the burrow.

Before Aldebaran set in the west,
Allegra and Lucy saw another pair of

polecats and one by itself. They returned to the cove delighted with what they'd seen. Fran was really pleased too.

'I was hoping there was more than one pair,' she said. 'That's great news.' She smiled at Lucy and Allegra. 'You must be longing to explore now.' She turned to her daughter. 'Tess, why don't you show Allegra and Lucy around?'

'OK,' Tess said, slightly reluctantly. She glanced at Lottie and Bea. 'Are you guys coming too?'

They nodded.

Ignoring Lucy, Tess turned to Allegra. 'Hey! Do you want to see the coolest place for doing magic round here?'

Allegra nodded. 'Yeah!'

Tess grinned at her. 'Come on then! It's this way!'

Tess flew out of the cove and up the cliff side. The others followed.

'Where are we going?' Lucy asked Lottie.

'It's a place called Carwyn's Rest,' Lottie replied. 'It's an ancient chamber built out of six huge stones. It's a brilliant place for doing magic, isn't it, Bea?'

Bea nodded shyly. She seemed much quieter than Lottie or Tess. 'Even I can do lots of magic there. I'm not brilliant at magic,' she explained to Lucy.

'You always say that,' Lottie told her. 'But you are good really.'

'Here we are!' Tess called.

Set back a little way from the cliff edge, Lucy could see some tall stones silhouetted against the starry sky. There were four upright ones and then two laid across them in a kind of a roof. Around the stones was an area of completely bare soil and just behind them was a copse of shadowy trees. Nearer the edge of the cliffs were some rabbit holes that Lucy guessed led into the polecats' warren.

As Lucy flew closer to the stones, a feeling of dread began to steal over her. Her heart beat faster. She felt very strange.

Tess and Allegra landed on the ground beside the standing stones. The stones towered above them, about three times the girls' height.

Lucy landed and looked round uneasily. 'This place feels weird.'

'Not scared, are you?' Tess challenged her.

'No,' Lucy said quickly. 'I . . . I just don't like it. It feels creepy.'

'Chicken,' mocked Tess.

'Actually I don't like it either,' Allegra put in.

Lucy noticed that Tess didn't tease Allegra. 'It's not that bad.' Tess shrugged. 'It just takes a while to get used to it. But when you do it's a great place for doing magic.'

'It feels . . .' Allegra hesitated, '. . . dark.'

'It's been used for dark magic in the past,' Tess told her.

'No one knows why it was originally built,' Bea put in, rather shyly. 'But one day, a long time ago, a dark stardust spirit called Morwenna began to use it. She wanted to be the most powerful stardust spirit ever and she magically bound and captured stardust spirits to help her draw down power directly from the stars.'

'Why did she need to use other spirits?' Lucy asked, horrified.

'Because stardust that is pulled down from the stars by magical force is so powerful that it wipes out the stardust of the person it is being pulled into. By getting the stardust to go through someone else, Morwenna kept her own powers and just added to them. If she'd drawn the power directly into herself it would have destroyed her,' Lottie explained.

'So she used other stardust spirits – they lost their stardust and could never turn into stardust spirits again,' Bea said. 'Morwenna became the most feared dark spirit ever, she had so much power.'

'Her magic gave her control of the

weather and the elements and even made people do her bidding too,' Tess added. 'She died eventually but ever since then this place has been a really powerful place for doing magic.' She pointed at the bare earth around it. 'People say that plants won't grow around it and animals won't come near it because of all the dark magic she did here.'

Lucy shivered. 'I don't like it.'

'Me neither,' said Allegra.

'I told you, you just need to get used to it,' Tess said. 'Go on, do some magic while you're here.' She looked directly at Lucy. 'Or maybe you're too scared?'

Lucy saw the challenge in Tess's eyes and lifted her chin. 'No. I'll do it.'

'You do something first,' Allegra said quickly to Tess.

'OK.' Tess hurried to the nearby copse and returned with some old dry twigs. 'Bet I can set fire to these,' she said putting the twigs into two piles inside the stone chamber.

Lucy blinked. From the way Tess had been behaving she'd thought she was about to do some serious magic. But then she remembered that most summer spirits their age could only heat things up and not actually set things alight. So starting off two fires was probably quite impressive.

'Want to see if I can do it?' Tess demanded.

Lucy shrugged. 'OK.'

Tess threw out her hand. 'Fire be

with me!' The two piles of sticks crackled and burst into flame. Tess looked triumphantly at Lucy. 'See.' She waved her hand. 'Fire be gone!'

The fires went out instantly.

'It's so cool how you can do that,' Bea said admiringly.

'Tess has been able to start fires since she was nine,' Lottie told Lucy. 'She's really powerful.'

Tess shot a smug look at Lucy. 'Your turn now. I'll fetch you some sticks.'

She fetched some wood and dumped it on the ground. 'Go on then!'

'Yeah, go on, Lucy,' Allegra said with a grin. 'See if you can do it.'

Lucy grinned back. 'Yes, let's see.' She stepped inside the ring of stones. An uneasy shiver ran down Lucy's spine but she ignored it and glanced upwards. Between the two stones that made up the roof, she could see the stars sparkling in the sky. They seemed to glow with power – all she had to do was let it come to her. A smile pulled at the corners of Lucy's mouth as she took a deep breath. This was going to be fun!

'Fire!' she said in a strong, commanding voice. 'Be with me!'

Power seemed to burst out of her and meet the power that was flooding down to her from the sky. Ignoring the pile of wood Tess had placed before her, she swung round in a rapid circle, pointing swiftly at six places just outside the standing stones. Six large balls of fire shot from her fingertips. As they landed they exploded upwards in six burning columns. For a moment, Lucy was too caught up in the feel of the magic beating through her to be surprised but as the shock on the others' faces on the other side of the fire gradually sank into her dazed brain she quickly waved her hands again. 'Fire be gone!'

The columns died down in a second, flickered and went out.

For a moment there was silence. The other four girls looked stunned.

'What did you do?' Bea whispered.

'You made six fires,' Lottie said as if she couldn't believe it.

'Six *columns* of fire,' Allegra breathed. 'Wow! I've never seen you do that before, Lucy.'

Lucy took a deep breath. Now that the power had stopped racing through her she felt empty and slightly faint. She hadn't meant to make the columns flare up like that; she'd just meant to make six fires. The magic had been so intense. She'd never felt anything like it before.

'You must be so powerful,' Bea said.

'That was amazing!' said Lottie.

Lucy glanced at Tess. 'That good enough for you?'

Tess swung round. 'I'm going back to the cove. Come on!' she snapped at Lottie and Bea.

She flew into the air. Lottie and Bea quickly followed her.

'Guess we should go too,' Allegra said to Lucy as they flew off.

Lucy looked into the inky shadows that surrounded the trees and suddenly gasped as something moved in the darkness. 'Allegra! Someone's there!'

Allegra caught sight of the movement too. She grabbed Lucy's arm. 'It's a person!'

Lucy felt as if someone had just tipped a bucket of icy water over her. A dark shape seemed to be forming and growing in the shadows . . .

CHAPTER
Three

'Quick, Lucy!' Allegra cried. 'Let's get away from here!'

They both shot up further into the sky.

'Who do you think it was?' Lucy said, her heart pounding.

'I bet it was a dark spirit!' Allegra replied. 'I felt really icy cold all of a sudden.'

'Me too,' Lucy said. They raced
through the air as fast as they could.
'We'd better tell your mum about it,'
Lucy said.

They found Xanthe near the cliffs.
When they told her about the
movements in the shadows, she looked
concerned. 'It made you feel very
cold?'

They nodded.

'And dizzy,' Allegra said.

Xanthe frowned. 'It might just have been your imaginations but I'll go and check it out. So what else did you get up to while you were there?'

'Well,' Lucy hesitated. 'I made these fires start . . .' She explained what had happened. 'I didn't mean to use powerful magic, it just happened,' she said apologetically.

To her relief, Xanthe looked slightly worried but not cross with her. 'Did anyone else apart from Tess, Lottie and Bea see?'

Lucy shook her head.

'It should be fine then. Tess knows about your powers. Fran and David told her. I can speak to Lottie and Bea and ask them not to tell the others. Be careful from now on though, Lucy.'

Lucy nodded. 'I will.'

The following morning, Lucy and Allegra woke up to find the sun streaming through the window. The sea was sparkling in the distance and the sky was blue. 'Look how sunny it is. I want to go down to the beach!' Allegra said.

'Me too,' Lucy agreed. They pulled on their clothes and hurried downstairs.

Xanthe and Fran were in the kitchen drinking coffee.

'Morning, girls,' Xanthe smiled.

'Hi! Can we go to the beach today?' Allegra asked eagerly.

'Of course. Tess is planning to go there with Lottie and Bea,' Fran said. 'Why don't you all go together?'

Lucy's heart sank. She'd far rather have gone just with Allegra but Fran was already going to the kitchen door. 'Tess!'

Tess came down the stairs. She smiled at Allegra but ignored Lucy.

'Allegra and Lucy want to go down to the beach this morning. What time are you meeting Lottie and Bea?'

'In half an hour,' Tess said.

'Great, well you can all go together then,' Fran said.

Tess didn't look too delighted but she nodded. 'OK.'

After breakfast, they all set off. Seagulls were flying overhead and there was a breeze blowing as they walked down the street.

'I do love it here!' Allegra said happily. 'You're so lucky to live by the sea, Tess.'

Tess smiled. 'I know. I'd hate to live anywhere else.'

Lucy turned to Allegra. 'I like living where we live. The woods are beautiful.'

'They're not like the sea though,' Tess said.

'They're just as nice,' Lucy retorted, feeling irritated.

'I'd far rather live by the sea,' Tess said.

'Well, I'd far rather live by the woods!' Lucy replied.

They glared at each other.

'Where are we meeting Lottie and Bea, Tess?' Allegra broke in quickly.

'At the end of the street.'

In front of them a small white bird swooped down and grabbed a bit of sandwich that someone had dropped on the pavement. 'Look at that seagull,' Lucy said.

'Its proper name is a kittiwake,' said Tess. 'Don't you know anything?'

Lucy felt her temper start to rise. 'Of course I do!'

Tess raised her eyebrows. 'You didn't even know what a polecat was.'

'So?' Lucy snapped. 'At least I can light more than two fires at once!'

Tess stiffened.

'Hey, look, guys, there's Lottie and Bea!' Allegra inetrrupted. 'Come on!'

Lucy and Tess gave each other angry looks but hurried after her. As they

reached Lottie and Bea, Allegra pulled
Lucy back a bit. 'What's got into you,
Luce? Are you determined to annoy
Tess today?'

'She's the annoying one!' Lucy
hissed.

'Give her a break,' Allegra said. 'It
must have been pretty embarrassing for
her yesterday when you lit all those
fires. You can tell she's used to everyone
here thinking she's really powerful.'

Just then, the others came over. 'Are
you coming down to the beach with
us?' Lottie asked.

'Yeah,' Allegra said.

'What should we do first?' Lottie
said to Tess.

'I'd like an ice cream,' Bea said.

'Let's save our money for later,' Tess

said bossily. 'We'll go and look at the rock pools first.'

Lucy felt a prickle of irritation as the others all nodded. Why did they have to do what Tess wanted? But she followed the others across the street towards the sands. Tess was talking to Allegra. Lucy hung back a bit. She looked round at the wide promenade. People were walking and jogging along it, children were kicking balls and there were various stalls selling jewellery or advertising things.

Lucy's attention was caught by a man in his twenties. He was setting up a stall and it had a picture of a polecat on. There was a large poster above the photo of the polecat that said 'Wildlife Watch! Can You Help?'

'Come on, Lucy,' Tess said as she and the others started walking down the steps on to the beach.

'Hang on. Look at this!' Lucy called.

'Later,' Tess said impatiently.

'Well, I want to look now!' Lucy said.

'You'll have to meet us down there then,' Tess said. 'Cos we're not waiting.'

'Come on, Lucy!' Allegra pleaded.

Lucy shook her head stubbornly. She wasn't going to do just what Tess wanted all the time. 'I'll catch you up.'

She turned back to the stall and looked at the picture again. The guy who was setting up the stand began pinning some more photos on the board. He was about medium height with dark spiky hair and brown eyes that sparkled in the morning sun. He had a blue T-shirt with a picture of a whale on. He looked round and noticed Lucy watching.

'Hello,' he said.

'What are you doing?' Lucy asked.

'I'm setting up a stand to tell people about polecats,' the guy replied. 'I'm a wildlife conservation officer. My name's Dan.'

'I'm Lucy,' she said.

'Are you interested in wildlife, Lucy?' Dan asked.

If only he knew! Lucy hid her grin. 'Yeah.'

'Well, maybe you can help me out then,' Dan told her. 'This is a polecat.' He pointed to the photo. 'They are very rare but there's been a couple of sightings of them on the cliff top recently and we're trying to find out more. We want people to tell us if they see any. If we find out where they're living we can protect them. So, if you're out and about, keep your eyes peeled and if you see any polecats let me know. We've got some information sheets here and a form for you to fill in.'

He handed Lucy a printed sheet.

'Here. It tells you how to spot a polecat.'

Lucy could barely contain herself. 'It's OK,' she said, the words tumbling out of her. 'I know all about polecats. They like living in empty rabbit warrens and in sandy dunes.'

'Have you seen any?' Dan looked very interested.

Lucy nodded. 'I saw some up on the cliffs near . . .' She frowned as she tried to remember the name of the place. '. . . Carwyn's Rest. I was there yesterday.'

Dan looked surprised. 'Yesterday?'

'Lucy!'

Lucy swung round. The others were coming up the steps towards her. 'What are you doing?' Allegra called.

57

'These are my friends,' Lucy told Dan. She turned to Allegra. 'This is Dan. He's a conservation officer. He's trying to find out about polecats.'

Dan nodded. 'We're setting up this stand here so that people can tell us if they see any.'

'Well . . .' Tess began but Dan had already turned back to Lucy again.

'You really saw some?' he said. 'Near Carwyn's Rest? How many? Was it in the evening?'

Lucy nodded. 'Yes, at . . .'

Tess quickly stepped on her foot. 'We were out for a walk with our parents. It was about sunset.'

Lucy glared at her. She knew Tess had only trodden on her foot to stop her saying something about being out late at night on their own. But she wasn't that stupid!

Dan hardly even glanced at Tess. 'So what did you see?' he asked Lucy intently.

'We were out with our parents,' she said, deciding to stick with Tess's story. 'It was just getting dark, and we saw five polecats on the cliff near the ancient chamber. There was a rabbit warren there that they came out of.'

'This is brilliant news!' Dan said, looking delighted. 'If you see them again let me know!'

'I will,' Lucy promised.

'Come on, let's go and get ice creams,' Tess said.

Lucy smiled at Dan and followed the others across the road. 'Isn't it weird

that he's looking for polecats! He's
really nice, isn't he?'

Tess shrugged. 'He's OK, I guess.'

Lucy was sure she was fed up that
she'd not been the centre of attention.

They went into the ice-cream
parlour. While the others were still
deciding Lucy and Allegra got their ice
creams and went outside.

'Tess is such a pain,' Lucy grumbled
as they sat on the low brick wall
outside the shop.

Allegra shot her a look. 'I bet you'd
really like her if you stopped arguing
with her all the time.'

'She's the one who argues with me,'
Lucy protested.

Allegra rolled her eyes. 'You're both as
bad as each other. In fact, I think that's

why you don't get on! You're too alike.'

'We are not!' Lucy exclaimed.

Just then Tess and the others came out of the ice-cream shop. 'What are you two talking about?' she asked curiously.

'Nothing,' Allegra said hastily.

'Well, come on,' Tess said. 'Let's go back down to the beach.'

Allegra jumped off the wall and followed her and the others.

With a sigh, Lucy went after them. 'I'm *not* like her,' she hissed, catching up with Allegra.

Allegra grinned but didn't say a word.

Four

'I am so *not* like Tess!' Lucy said for about the hundredth time as she and Allegra flew to the stardust cove that night.

'You so are,' Allegra told her. She twirled upwards in the air. 'You're both stubborn, I mean determined,' she corrected herself quickly as she saw the look on Lucy's face. 'You're both really competitive and you both . . .' She hesitated. '. . . like being in charge.'

'I don't!' Lucy protested. 'Come on! It's this way!'

They swooped down into the cove.

Fran waved to them. Tess, Lottie and Bea were already with her. 'Hi, you two,' she said. 'Will you work with Bea and Lottie tonight? There are some skylarks nesting in the rough fields up by Bronwen's Peak. They are very rare, shy birds and I don't want their nests to be disturbed, so I'd like you to work out how to keep inquisitive people and animals away while the eggs hatch.'

Lucy and the others nodded.

'What about me?' Tess asked.

'I'd like you to work with Molly, Lloyd and Jason tonight,' Fran told her.

'I want you to check out how many kittiwakes are nesting on the cliffs at Crescent Bay.'

'Can't I go with Lottie and the others?' Tess protested.

'It's good for you to learn to work with different people,' Fran told her.

Looking fed up, Tess flew to join Lloyd, Molly and Jason, three slightly older stardust spirits.

Lottie and Bea showed Lucy and Allegra the way to Bronwen's Peak where the skylarks were nesting.

The nests were in hollows on the ground. Lucy had never seen a bird nesting on the ground before. 'Why don't they nest in trees?'

'They just don't,' Bea told her. 'They always use the ground.' She looked at the small brown birds. 'They look ordinary but they sing beautifully.'

Lottie looked around. 'We need to try and make sure that people don't come to this bit of the field. We can't grow anything too close to the birds though because they like open land for nesting in.'

'Why don't we grow a line of bramble bushes cutting off this corner of the field?' Allegra suggested.

'We could,' Lottie said. 'But I don't know if Bea and I have got enough power to grow a whole line of bushes.'

'I can only normally grow one and then I get tired.' Bea said apologetically. 'I'm not very good at growing things.'

'Well, why don't you try and see,' Lucy suggested.

'I suppose I could,' Bea said doubtfully. She held out her hand. 'Grow anew!' she declared. On the patch of grass where she was pointing a bramble bush began to grow out of the ground.

Lottie did the same.

'That's great!' Lucy exclaimed. 'Now

we just need some more to cut off this end of the field.'

'I'll never be able to grow enough of them,' Bea said. 'It's a good idea though. Maybe we should go and get some of the adults to help.'

'No way!' Allegra said. 'We can do this on our own. You just need more power.'

'But how do we get more power?' Lottie said.

'Lucy.' Allegra grinned.

'Me?' Lucy said.

'Yes,' Allegra told her. 'You know how Xanthe said that magic's attracted to you? Well, all you have to do is let it flow into you, then if Bea and Lottie are holding your hands I bet the magic will flow from you into them.'

'Hang on,' Lucy said quickly. 'Isn't that what that dark spirit Morwenna did?'

'This is different,' Allegra replied quickly. 'I've seen Xanthe do it with some of the other adults back in our woods when they're trying to work magic together. You're not forcing magic to come to you by saying a magic spell. You're just allowing it to flow into you and then out again to do magic. The thing about Morwenna was that she was keeping all the stardust inside herself. You'll be letting stardust flow into you then out into Lottie and Bea. They'll use it to do their magic to help nature and any that is left over will just flow back up to the stars. It's OK to use magic in that way – in fact it's good.'

Lucy considered it for a moment. It did seem to make sense. 'All right. Let's do it.'

'I really think we should get the other adults,' Bea said nervously. 'It would be a lot safer.'

Allegra grinned. 'But nowhere near as much fun! Come on, Lucy!'

Lucy wasn't quite sure what she had to do. Taking a deep breath she closed her eyes for a moment. As she let the breath out she looked up at the stars. They glittered like fairy lights above her. She began to trace the patterns in the sky – the two bears, the lynx, the dragon and then Leo the lion – the constellation of the summer spirits. The Royal Star, Regulus, was glowing brightly in the lion's chest.

The Royal Stars were four of the brightest stars in the sky. Each type of stardust spirit got their stardust from a different Royal Star, which is why they could do different types of magic. As Lucy stared at Regulus she could almost see the magic crackling across the sky. Her skin tingled.

'Hold my hands,' she breathed to Lottie and Bea. The lion shape seemed to stand out, to grow brighter as she watched. Warmth flooded through Lucy. She was vaguely aware of Lottie and Bea giving little gasps of surprise but she kept her eyes on the lion. She could feel the power flowing into her, she welcomed it, let it flow through her and out into them. Every nerve in her body sang. She felt as if she could do anything in the world.

'Go on!' she heard Allegra urge the others.

'Grow anew!' Lottie and Bea both gasped beside her.

Lucy felt the power surge even more strongly. *Magic*, she thought in delight, losing herself in the feeling.

'That's it!' Allegra exclaimed after a few minutes. 'Lucy! We've done it! You can stop now!'

Stop now. The words seemed to echo in Lucy's head. Feeling like she was swimming upwards from the depths of a swimming pool she gradually became aware of Lottie and Bea holding her hands, of the solid ground beneath her feet, the night air cool on her face. She

blinked and the power stopped. 'Wow!'
she breathed.

Lottie and Bea looked stunned. 'That
was . . . that was . . . it was just . . .'
Lottie trailed off, lost for words.

Lucy looked at the field. There was
now a line of bramble bushes blocking
off the skylarks' corner of the field.

'It worked,' she said.

'Brilliantly!' Allegra grinned. 'What did it feel like? It looked cool.'

'It was just amazing,' Bea breathed, her eyes wide. 'I've never felt anything like it.'

Lottie stared at Lucy. 'How did you do it?'

'I don't know,' Lucy said. 'The magic just flowed into me and then into you.'

'Then back into nature just as it should,' Allegra said happily.

Lucy walked forward and stretched. As she did so, icy fingers seemed to run down her spine. She swung round. She had the strangest feeling that she was being watched.

'What is it?' Allegra said, seeing her face.

Lucy's eyes scanned the darkness of
the fields around them. Nothing
moved. All was still. But she still had
the creepiest feeling that they weren't
alone.

'Lucy?' Allegra said.

'I . . . I just felt weird for a moment.'
Lucy glanced around again. 'Come on,'
she said uneasily. 'Let's not stay here
any longer. We've done what we had
to do.'

The others nodded. As Lucy took
off into the air she glanced quickly
down at the empty fields. There was
nothing there. Nothing to be scared of.

So why did she feel there was?

When they got back to the cove they
found Tess waiting. The words tumbled

out of Lottie and Bea as they began to
tell Tess everything that had happened.

'I've never felt so powerful!' Bea
gasped.

'Lucy's amazing!' said Lottie.

'It was Allegra's idea,' Lucy said
modestly. 'I didn't think of it.'

'But you were the one who did it,'
Allegra told her.

'You should have been with us, Tess,'
Bea put in. 'It was –'

'Yeah, great. I get it!' Tess snapped.
'But it *was* dangerous. You shouldn't
have tried to channel magic like that.
Not without an adult there.'

Lucy suddenly found herself feeling
sorry for Tess. She imagined how she
would feel if Allegra was to go off and
have lots of fun doing magic with

other people. She knew she'd hate it.
She changed the subject. 'What shall
we do now?'

'I don't know!' Tess said grumpily.
'You can think of something seeing as
you're so clever.'

'Tess . . .' Lucy began, reaching out
to touch the other girl's arm.

Tess pulled quickly away.

'Xanthe's coming!' Lottie said
warningly.

Xanthe walked over. 'Is everything
OK, girls?'

'Yeah, everything's fine,' Allegra said
quickly.

Tess and Lucy didn't say anything.

'So how have you all got on this
evening?' Xanthe asked, looking at
them thoughtfully.

'Really well,' Allegra replied. 'Lucy channelled some power from the sky.'

'Really?' Xanthe said. 'What happened?'

Allegra, Lottie and Bea explained. Lucy wondered for a moment if Xanthe would be cross with her but Xanthe looked pleased. 'That was a very clever use of your gift for channelling magic, Lucy. Well done.'

Tess sighed loudly as if she was bored.

Lucy shot her a look.

Xanthe looked at the two of them. 'Well, I think you've all done enough for tonight,' she said smoothly. 'So why don't you just go and have some fun? Tomorrow, you'll be working in pairs.'

Lucy looked at Allegra. 'That'll be fun!'

'Yes,' Xanthe agreed. 'I think Allegra, you can go with Bea. Lottie, you can pair up with Molly from the other group, and Lucy and Tess . . .' She gave them a bright smile. 'I think you two can work together.'

Five

'I can't believe your mum!' Lucy exclaimed to Allegra as soon as they were alone. 'Why do I have to work with Tess? She doesn't want to be with me any more than I want to be with her!'

Tess had flown off with the others. She hadn't said a word in front of Xanthe but she'd looked totally fed up.

'It won't be that bad,' Allegra said sympathetically.

'It will,' declared Lucy.

'Well, there's no point stressing about it now,' Allegra said sensibly. 'Let's go and look at the polecats.'

Lucy cheered up a bit at the thought. 'OK. If we find out any more about them we can tell Dan at his stand tomorrow!'

Allegra and Lucy spotted a new polecat that night. Lucy was delighted and couldn't wait to tell Dan. She and Allegra saw him up on the cliffs the next day when they were out exploring.

'Hi, Dan!' Lucy called, running over with Allegra.

Dan straightened up. 'Hi, girls. Have
you seen any more polecats?'

'Yes, we saw another one last night,'
Lucy said.

Allegra nodded. 'That's six now.'

Dan grinned. 'I can see you two
are going to be my star polecat
spotters!'

Lucy grinned, feeling very pleased.

Just then a group of teenage boys
came walking up the footpath. They
were shoving and pushing each other
and laughing. As they walked past Dan,
the boy in front chucked his empty
Coke can on the ground.

'Hey!' Dan said.

The boys ignored him.

Dan stepped in front of them. 'Can
you pick that up, please?' he said levelly.

'You what?' the one who had dropped the can said.

'Pick it up,' Dan repeated.

A few of the other boys sniggered. 'You do it,' the boy said.

Lucy looked nervously at Dan. What was he going to do?

But Dan didn't look worried. He fixed his eyes on the boy's face and spoke very quietly but firmly. 'Pick it up.'

Lucy thought the boy was going to reply rudely but as he met Dan's eyes his face changed and he suddenly nodded meekly. 'OK,' he said, picking the can up. 'Sorry. I'll find a bin.'

'That's great!' Dan said, a smile instantly spreading across his face. 'I knew you'd see it my way.'

Looking rather stunned, the boy
carried on his way, the crumpled can in
his hands. The others followed him
looking equally stunned.

Dan watched them go. 'I wish people like that wouldn't come up here on the cliff top. They only cause trouble, damaging the wildlife and leaving litter. I wish more people were like you and your friends,' he said, 'interested in wildlife and the environment.'

'We love stuff like that,' Lucy said, glancing at Allegra. 'Don't we?'

Allegra grinned. 'We do.'

'Well, keep looking out for those polecats,' Dan told them.

'We will,' Lucy promised. 'See you soon.'

'Yeah,' he said. 'Soon.'

Lucy and Allegra spent most of the day hanging out on the cliffs and the promenade. Whenever Lucy thought about the night ahead of them she groaned inside. Working with Tess was going to be awful.

Hopefully we can get the task done as soon as possible, she thought.

Fran told them that she wanted them to clear an area of heathland that had become overgrown. She flew with them to the place to show them what she wanted them to do.

They landed on a piece of the heath that was covered in gorse bushes.

'All this gorse is no good for the wildlife and other plants,' Fran said. 'It stops birds like skylarks and choughs from being able to nest on the ground and it smothers plants that butterflies and damselflies need to lay their eggs on. I want you to clear it.'

Lucy looked round at the gorse. 'But how do we do that?'

Tess spoke. 'We use fire, don't we, Mum? It burns the gorse and then the plants underneath can regrow.'

'Fire!' Lucy echoed. She had used fire in the woods at home to burn dead branches away but she knew how dangerous it could be to set fires in open areas of heathland. There were signs everywhere warning that fires could spread very quickly in open areas like this.

Fran must have noticed her unease. 'It would be dangerous if you were human, but you two are both powerful enough stardust spirits to be able to keep a fire under control now. Keep the fires small and use magical shields to contain the fires. Work together and you'll be fine. Tess is very good at casting magical shields and Xanthe says you're excellent at controlling fire, Lucy. I'm only going to be a short distance away so if there are any problems come to fetch me straight away.' She smiled at them encouragingly. 'I'm sure you can do this, girls.'

She flew off and Lucy and Tess were left alone together.

'I guess we get started then,' Tess said. 'I'll cast a protective barrier in a circle and you start a fire in the middle. The fire should burn up to the barrier and then not be able to go any further. You can put the fire out and then we can move on. Let's start in the middle and burn outwards.'

Lucy bristled at Tess's bossy tone. 'No, let's start at the edge of the cliff top and burn inwards.'

Tess frowned at her. 'Don't be dumb. We're going to start in the middle. That's the way we always do it here.'

Lucy glowered at her but reluctantly accepted that she'd never done this before whereas Tess had. 'OK,' she muttered.

'Shield be with me,' Tess breathed. She swung her arm in a circle and a magical barrier formed in the gorse about two metres wide. It was almost invisible, only a faint shimmering light showing where it was.

'Start your fire in the middle,' Tess

instructed. 'You'll need to make it strong.'

Lucy sighed in irritation. 'Fire be with me!' She pointed to the centre of the circle. But she'd forgotten how powerfully her magic worked in Pembrokeshire. Flames exploded, filling the whole circle.

With a gasp, Tess jumped back. In her shock, she lost her concentration and the barrier vanished. The flames leapt outwards, devouring the surrounding gorse bushes. The bushes crackled and snapped as they burnt.

'Lucy!' Tess exclaimed.

Coughing and spluttering, Lucy quickly called out, 'Fire be gone.' The flames extinguished immediately.

The two girls stared at the blackened

circle of land. The gorse bushes had burnt to the ground in a five-metre-wide circle.

'That was way too big a fire, Lucy!' Tess exclaimed angrily. 'What a stupid thing to do!'

'You were the one who told me it
had to be strong!' Lucy retorted guiltily.
'Anyway your barrier wasn't much use.'

'That's because I wasn't expecting
you to start a fire that big!' Tess
shouted.

'Right, well next time I won't!'

They glared at each other.

'Should we do this bit next?' Lucy
snapped, pointing to the next area.

Tess nodded curtly. She cast a shield.
Lucy made a fire in the middle of it
but it was no use. They just seemed
incapable of working together.
Whenever Lucy's fires got big enough
to start burning the gorse properly Tess
squashed them with her barrier so they
only managed to burn a tiny bit of
gorse at a time. In the end Lucy got so

fed up that she made a really strong
fire flame up and once again it burnt a
much bigger area than she'd intended.

'Lucy!' Tess shouted in exasperation,
as she jumped back to avoid being
burnt by burning bits of gorse that
were flying into the air.

Lucy stopped the fire. Her throat
was sore from the smoke and her eyes
itched. 'This is stupid! We're never
going to get this done.'

'Well, it's not my fault!' Tess snapped.

'It's not mine either!' Lucy replied.
'I'm going back to the cove.'

'Me too,' Tess retorted.

Without saying another word to
each other the girls rose into the sky.
As they approached the cliff top where
Carwyn's Rest stood, Tess swooped

high above it. Lucy began to follow her but just then her eyes caught a movement in the darkness surrounding the stones. What was it?

She stared. A figure wearing a dark cloak with a hood was hurrying out of the shadows of the trees towards the stone chamber!

CHAPTER
Six

Lucy was so shocked she almost forgot to fly.

The figure approaching the chamber stopped as if it had sensed something.

Camouflagus! Lucy thought. As her body vanished against the starry background, the figure looked up sharply.

Lucy flew upwards as fast as she

could. She could see Tess in the
distance about to fly over the cliff and
down to the beach. Their argument
vanished from her mind. She raced
towards her. 'Tess!' she hissed. 'There's
someone by Carwyn's Rest! I can't see
if it's a man or a woman – they're
wearing a hood.'

Tess stared. 'Really?'

'Yes!' Lucy exclaimed. 'Come and see
but camouflage yourself. I got a really
horrible sick feeling when I saw them.
Maybe it's a dark spirit!'

She wondered if Tess would want
to go back to the cove and fetch the
adults but Tess just nodded. 'OK.'
She quickly camouflaged herself and
together they flew back to the
standing stones.

'Where?' Tess hissed.

Lucy looked round. The figure had gone.

'There's no one there,' Tess said.

'There must be!' Lucy hissed. She looked round feeling very uneasy. Where had the figure gone? 'Maybe they've camouflaged themselves,' she whispered.

'Or maybe there was no one there at all,' Tess said crossly.

'Tess!' Lucy said as Tess flew away. 'There *was* someone there,' she said, flying after her. 'I'm not making it up!'

Tess looked angrily at Lucy. 'You shouldn't joke about dark spirits, Lucy. They're not funny.'

'I wasn't joking!' Lucy protested.

Xanthe was on the beach when they

got back. Lucy quickly told her what she'd thought she'd seen.

'I'll look into it,' Xanthe promised. 'But maybe you just imagined this figure, Lucy. Those burial stones have so much magic surrounding them they can make people imagine things. How did you get on with your task?'

When Lucy and Tess admitted that they hadn't succeeded in getting rid of the gorse, Xanthe was not very pleased.

'I'm disappointed in the pair of you,' she said. 'You really should have been able to do a simple task like that by working together. Tomorrow I'd like you to finish off burning the gorse, and see if you can manage better. Now off you go.'

Looking rather red in the face, Tess

flew away. Lucy turned to go too.

'Lucy,' Xanthe said stopping her. 'It really *is* important that you learn to work with lots of different people. You're used to working in a team with people who have different powers than you but being able to work with people with the same powers is just as important. By combining your magic, your power will increase. Your similarity will give you strength. Will you try your best to work with Tess tomorrow?'

Lucy sighed. 'Yes.'

'Good girl,' Xanthe smiled.

Lucy flew to the next bay where Allegra was watching the polecats play.

'Hi! How did it go with Tess?' Allegra called.

'Not well,' Lucy replied, with a sigh. 'We . . .'

She broke off as a high-pitched animal squeal echoed through the night air.

'What's that?' Lucy exclaimed.

'I don't know!' Allegra said.

There was a second squeal. 'It sounds like an animal in pain – or one who's really scared,' Allegra said in alarm.

'It's coming from the cliff top!' Lucy exclaimed. 'Quick! Let's find out what's going on!'

Lucy and Allegra flew into the air. An image of the hooded figure flashed into Lucy's mind. But then the animal screamed again – a sound of pure terror – and forgetting everything but the need to help, Lucy raced to the cliff top with Allegra.

'Look!' Allegra gasped, pointing at the stone chamber. In the centre of them was a metal trap. A polecat was caught inside it. It was racing round the small metal box, its ears flattened against its head, its eyes wide and frantic. It opened its mouth and screamed again.

'Poor thing!' Allegra cried. She flew to the trap. Landing beside it she began to try and open the door at the back to let the polecat out. 'It's OK,' she soothed the terrified animal. 'We'll get you out!'

Lucy crouched down as Allegra's fingers worked at the stiff bolts on the cage. 'There now, little one,' she soothed the frightened animal. 'You'll be all right.' The polecat seemed to

listen. It stopped running round the
cage and looked at them with wide
eyes. Lucy looked around. Was this the
work of the hooded figure?

'Almost done,' Allegra said. She
pulled one bolt back. 'There!' she said
as she undid the second. The door
opened and the polecat bounded out,

its dark-brown coat gleaming in the starlight as it raced outside the stones.

'I wonder who put the trap there,' Lucy said.

'At least it wasn't the sort of trap that kills animals.' Allegra shuddered. 'Poor thing. Just being trapped must have been scary enough.'

'He seems OK now,' Lucy said, but as she spoke the polecat froze. It stared into the copse behind the stones, and then with a squeal of fear it turned and raced into a burrow.

'What's it doing?' Lucy said, and then she gasped as an icy wave seemed to sweep over her. 'A-Allegra,' she stammered.

'Yeah.' Allegra's voice quavered. 'I don't feel so good.'

'Me neither.' Lucy felt sick and faint. Something seemed to be moving in the shadows of the trees. The coldness pressed closer.

'Mum!' Allegra gasped suddenly.

Lucy opened her eyes. Xanthe was flying through the sky towards them.

'What was that noise?' she said looking very worried.

'A polecat.' Lucy looked round. The sick feeling was fading now and the shadows were still again. 'Caught in a trap.'

'But who would do such a thing?' Xanthe said, sounding puzzled. 'Gamekeepers put traps out but they wouldn't set a trap up here on the cliff top.'

'It was really frightened,' Allegra said.

'It sounded terrified,' Xanthe said. She began to investigate the area inside the stones. 'Oh, no,' she murmured.

Lucy had a feeling of dread. 'What is it?'

Xanthe turned slowly and showed them what she was holding – dark-brown animal fur that looked like it had come from a polecat and a small clay jar that was full of earth.

'What are they?' Lucy asked in astonishment.

'Aren't they the kind of things that are used in dark magic rituals?' Allegra asked in alarm.

Xanthe looked more worried than Lucy had ever seen her look before. 'Yes. They are. This looks like the work of a dark spirit.' She glanced round. 'Come on,' she said urgently. 'I don't think we should stay here any longer.'

Lucy didn't sleep well that night. Her dreams were filled with images of the ancient chamber. She was stuck in the centre and she couldn't move. Around the outside of the stones, the shadows were pressing in towards her. The air seemed to tremble with darkness – a darkness that was getting closer and closer . . .

Lucy woke with a start, her heart pounding. It was a relief to see the early-morning sun shining into the room through the half-shut curtains. Shaking her head to try and rid her

mind of the dream, Lucy padded over
to the window.

In the distance the sea was glittering
a deep blue and in the cornflower-blue
sky there were fluffy white clouds and
seagulls swooping through the air. Lucy
leant against the window ledge. It was
such a peaceful scene but she just
couldn't feel calm. It was as though
there was something bubbling away
under the surface, something really bad.

She pressed her head against the
cool glass of the windowpane.
Something was going on and it had
something to do with the stone
chamber. But what? Had a dark spirit
really been there?

She jumped suddenly as a hand
touched her arm. Turning round, she

saw it was Allegra. Lucy had been so deep in thought that she hadn't heard her getting out of bed.

'You OK?' Allegra asked, looking at her with concern.

'Not really,' Lucy sighed. 'I really think there might be a dark spirit nearby.'

'Yes,' Allegra said. 'I felt it yesterday too.'

'Do you think they were going to use the polecat they trapped?' Lucy said, feeling sick.

Allegra frowned. 'I've heard Xanthe say that animals don't attract stardust in the same way people do. I don't know why the polecat was there with the other things. It doesn't make sense.'

'Nothing makes sense,' Lucy sighed.

Allegra squeezed her arm. 'It'll be OK, Luce. The adults will deal with it.'

Lucy gazed out of the window. She didn't want to think about horrible creepy things any more. 'I wish we could see some dolphins.'

'Me too,' Allegra agreed. 'There were loads here last time I came. Why don't we walk along the cliff top after breakfast and see if we can spot any?'

'OK,' Lucy agreed. 'Let's!'

After breakfast, Lucy and Allegra hurried out of the house. 'I'm glad Tess couldn't come,' Lucy said. Tess had a dentist's appointment that morning. 'It's nice just being the two of us.' She sighed. 'I wish I could work with you tonight, not Tess.'

'You'd better get the gorse burnt tonight though or Xanthe and Fran will be really cross,' Allegra said.

Lucy nodded. 'It's just so hard trying to work with her.' She saw a familiar figure walking along the cliff top. 'Hey, there's Dan! Let's go and say hello!'

They ran to meet him.

'Hi, Dan!' Lucy called.

'Hello.' For once the conservation officer didn't smile.

Lucy looked at him in surprise. 'Are you OK?'

'Sorry. I didn't mean to be rude,' Dan said. 'I'm just angry this morning.'

'Why?' Lucy asked.

Dan ran a hand through his spiky hair. 'Someone's been trying to trap polecats. I found a trap up on the cliffs by the burial chamber. Luckily it was empty, but it just makes me really mad. They're not harming anyone living up here.'

'I know!' Lucy burst out. 'I mean, I

know the polecats aren't doing any harm up here,' she added quickly.

'Who do you think might have set the trap?' Allegra asked Dan.

'Oh, it's bound to be teenagers messing around,' Dan replied. 'We often get groups of them going to the standing stones in the evening – they make a mess, start fires. It's bound to be them.'

Allegra frowned. 'But why would a group of teenagers want to trap a polecat?'

'Who knows?' Dan turned away from her and directed his words to Lucy. 'I just *wish* there was some way of protecting the polecats – that there was some way of guarding them at night, particularly Carwyn's Rest. That's where the teenagers always hang out. But I can't stay up all night.'

Lucy's eyes widened. She saw an identical expression on Allegra's face and was sure they'd had the exact same idea. Dan might not be able to stay up all night to guard them but they could! They'd guarded honey buzzards from people before back at home. They could ask Fran if they could watch over the polecats. Surely she would say yes.

Lucy looked back at Dan. 'I bet the teenagers won't cause you any more trouble,' she said.

'I wish I could share your confidence,' Dan sighed. 'Well, we'll see. I'd better go now, girls. Have a good day!'

'Bye!' they called.

As soon as he was a safe distance away Lucy looked at Allegra. 'Were you thinking what I was thinking?' she whispered.

'That we should guard the polecats tonight?'

Lucy nodded. 'Whoever's setting those traps, we'll make sure they never do it again!'

CHAPTER

Seven

'I'm sorry girls but the answer's no,'
Fran said to Lucy and Allegra that
night.

'But why?' Lucy protested in surprise.

'I don't want you near Carwyn's
Rest – not until we know more about
what's going on there,' Fran replied.
'You know what Xanthe found there
last night.'

'But what about the polecats?'
Allegra protested.

'Don't worry,' Fran replied. 'I've
already checked that there are no traps
and Bethan and Mark are going to
keep an eye on the cliff path – if it is
teenagers who set the trap yesterday
they'll come that way.' She looked at
the girls' worried faces. 'It will be OK,'
she said gently. 'Now, you need to get
your tasks done quickly this evening
because later on tonight we're all going
to Guillemot Island. It's a bird
sanctuary. We fly to it once month to
check that everything is OK there.
Allegra, I'd like you and Bea to check
the skylarks. Lucy, I want you to work
with Tess again to try and get that
gorse cleared.'

Lucy sighed.

Fran looked at her. 'I hope you two manage to make more progress tonight. Go and find Tess, off you go!'

Lucy flew off. Tess was hanging out with Lottie and Bea by the cliffs. 'We've got to go and do gorse,' Lucy told her reluctantly.

Tess didn't look any keener than Lucy. 'OK,' she sighed. 'See you guys later,' she said to Lottie and Bea.

Neither Tess nor Lucy said a word to each other until they reached the gorse-covered cliff top.

The circles they had burnt the night before were clearly visible. Lucy's heart sank as she looked round at the amount of gorse they still had to burn.

'We've got to get this done quickly,'

Tess said. 'If we're here all night, we'll miss the trip.'

For once they were in agreement. Lucy nodded. She wanted to get it over and done with as soon as possible. 'Let's get started.'

But it was much easier said than done. Just like the night before they couldn't seem to get their magic to work together; either Lucy's fires were too strong to be contained by Tess's barriers or Tess's barriers put out Lucy's fires. It took them ages.

After a couple of hours Tess stopped and looked round. 'Do you think that'll do?'

Lucy looked round. They had burnt about three quarters of the gorse but it wasn't very evenly done. There were patches of bushes sticking up all over the blackened heath and not all the gorse bushes they had set fire to had burnt all the way to the ground. But she was so fed up and longing to stop that she nodded. 'Yeah, it'll be fine.'

They glanced at each other.

'If they think it's not good enough they can always make us come back tomorrow to finish off,' Tess said as if trying to convince herself.

Lucy nodded. 'We've done loads tonight.'

Tess flew into the sky. Lucy followed but made no attempt to catch her up. It wasn't as if they were going to talk to each other. She'd rather fly on her own.

They swooped over the fields. When

they reached Carwyn's Rest, Tess stayed
well away, taking a longer route round
the edge of the heath to avoid flying
near it. However, Lucy couldn't stop
thinking about the polecats and she
flew closer. *Maybe I could just fly down
really quickly and check them*, she
thought.

She dived towards the stones but as she drew closer she felt her skin start to prickle. She looked down. The trees were shadowy and dark but in the centre of the stone chamber she could see a faint flickering light. What was it?

She flew down. In the centre of the chamber someone had lit a small fire. Lucy stared. Who would have done that? Suddenly she seemed to hear Dan's words in her head: *teenagers . . . they leave litter, light fires . . .*

Maybe some teenagers had come to try and trap a polecat again.

Lucy raced after Tess.

'Tess! Wait!'

Tess was just about to fly over the cliff. 'What is it?'

'There's a fire in the chamber! I

think there are some teenagers trying to trap the polecats. Come on! Let's go and see what's going on!'

'I'm not going back there! You know my mum said we weren't supposed to!' Tess exclaimed.

'But maybe someone's trying to hurt the polecats,' Lucy said.

Tess hesitated but then shook her head. 'We should go and get some adults if you're worried.'

'There might not be time!' Lucy cried. 'Let's go!'

Tess looked torn but then shook her head. 'No.'

'Fine,' Lucy said angrily, wishing it was Allegra with her not Tess. 'I'll go on my own!' And she flew off.

Flying as fast as she could she raced

back towards Carwyn's Rest. The
shadows around the stones looked darker
than ever. Lucy's eyes scanned around.
There was no sign of any movement.
She flew lower; she could see the polecat
burrows but there were no obvious traps.

She looked at the ancient chamber
with the flickering fire. Suddenly she
realized there were other objects on the
floor of the chamber. What were they?

Heart beating loudly in her chest,
she landed and walked between the
stones. Her heart skipped a beat.

In the centre of the stones, someone
had traced a circle around the fire with
a white powder that looked like chalk.
Placed around the circle were three
different objects: a silver bowl filled
with water, an empty glass bottle with

a stopper in and then a small pot filled with earth just like Xanthe had found the night before.

Lucy's mouth felt dry. Earth, air, fire and water. The four elements that stardust spirits used in their magic. What was going on? A branch on the ground outside the stones cracked.

Someone was coming!

The flickering firelight made the shadows around the chamber even darker. She felt faint. *I've got to get away from here!* The thought drummed into her head. She rose up into the air and then suddenly jerked to a stop.

It was as though a giant iron hand had suddenly grabbed her. She couldn't move! Magic was holding her there. She was caught fast!

'Help!' she shouted.

A hooded figure stepped out of the shadows and into the burial chamber. From under the cloak, a hand was pointing at Lucy.

A dark spirit! Great waves of fear and sickness rolled over Lucy. She tried to fight against them.

'Who are you?' she gasped.

The person threw their head back. The black hood fell down revealing their face.

'Dan!' Lucy exclaimed, feeling totally confused. 'What are you doing here?'

But even as she spoke, Dan began to change – his skin became old, his hair thinned and turned grey and his twinkling eyes became dull, the whites turning yellow, as they sank into deep hollows in his now wrinkled face.

'No!' Lucy whispered, horror racing through her.

'Yes, Lucy.' Dan's voice rang with power. 'This is me. The real me!'

Lucy tried to fight through the faintness in her head. How could this be? 'But you can't be a dark spirit. I've never felt ill around you before.'

'Ah, that is because my coven of dark spirits has been drawing magic down from the skies and using it to create powerful magic. Magic that hides our true nature from other stardust spirits whenever we choose. It gives us so much power!' He smiled in delight. 'We can visit any stardust group we like without them knowing a thing. Find spirits. Take their stardust.'

Lucy's stomach felt as if it was filled with icy water. 'Is that what you're going to do to me?'

Dan looked at her. 'You are no ordinary stardust spirit, Lucy. It is very rare to find someone who can channel magic so easily. I have been watching you. I saw the fires you made the first night; I saw the way you channelled power and used it to help your friends with their magic.' He circled round her. 'Stardust loves you, Lucy. It flows into you. It transforms the small amount of power that you have inside you to something so much bigger.'

Lucy frowned. *He's wrong*, she thought. *I don't just draw power from the stars. The power inside me isn't small — it's real power. I know it.*

Dan started speaking again. 'You are going to help me become the most powerful dark spirit alive today. You will be my stardust sacrifice!'

Lucy stared at him in horror as she realized what he was going to do. 'You want to use me to draw power from the sky so it can flow into you?'

'Yes,' Dan said, his sunken eyes

glittering in the firelight. 'I had other plans for gaining power but I no longer need them. You have come to me like a gift from the stars. By using you in a stardust ritual, I will be able to draw down more power than anyone has before. I will be able to control the weather, bend people to my will, use my magic as much in the day as well as at night. I will also reclaim that which has been lost to the stardust world for too long.'

'What will happen to me?' Lucy whispered, her throat dry.

'The power will flow through you into me and, in doing so, your own stardust will be destroyed,' Dan said.

He clenched his fist and pulled his arm towards his chest.

Lucy felt herself being pulled through the air towards him. 'No!' she exclaimed, struggling.

Dan's power-hungry eyes bored into hers. 'Yes,' he hissed. 'There is no escape!'

Eight

Lucy tried to break free but Dan's magic was too strong. He brought her down to the ground until she was standing in the middle of the chalk circle, then he muttered a few words and suddenly she found her arms clapped to her sides. It was as though he had wrapped her body in iron ropes.

'You won't get away with it!' Lucy
gasped. 'The other stardust spirits will
come to find me!'

'No, they won't,' Dan told her. 'I
took care of that last night. When I
placed the jar of earth and the polecat
fur here, I knew the adults would fear
dark magic at work and forbid anyone
to come here until they had learnt

more. And it is the night of their silly
trip so no one will come, Lucy. The
ritual *will* take place. This was meant to
be.'

His words slammed into Lucy and
she knew he was right. Tears pricked at
her eyes. 'I thought you were nice!' she
whispered.

'That's because I *wanted* you to think
that,' Dan told her coldly. 'I became
someone I knew you would like.'

'So you don't really care about
wildlife at all?'

'Not really,' Dan agreed. 'I used the
polecats to get to you.'

'*You* trapped that polecat last night!'
Lucy said.

Dan nodded. 'I knew that if you
found it, it would bring you to me

tonight. How could you resist the chance to help a defenceless creature?' He put on his old, kind Dan voice. '*I just wish there was some way of protecting the polecats – but I can't stay up all night,*' he said, repeating his words from earlier in that day. Then he grinned evilly. 'Oh, Lucy, it's been so easy to make you do what I wanted.'

Anger fired through Lucy again. 'Well, I'm not going to do it now!' she shouted, struggling furiously against her magic bonds.

Dan's voice rose. 'You have no choice!' He began to move round the circle, moving each object just inside the chalk line. 'Once the ritual has been started, it cannot be stopped. The magic will gather in the skies until it is so strong it will strike down to this circle. If it doesn't flow into you it will hit the ground like a lightning bolt and its power will destroy everything in the ground in the area – plants, insects, animals . . .'

'The polecats?' Lucy whispered.

'They will die if someone is not in the circle to take the power,' Dan said.

Lucy stared at him. 'I hate you!'

'I know.' He met her eyes. 'But you cannot stop me!'

Throwing up his arms, he turned to the skies. The starlight fell on his face, making it look more wrinkled than ever. He began to recite a spell. Lucy did not understand the words but the sound of them made her skin crawl as if ants were running over it. They were old –

ancient – and they seemed to make the very air in the stone chamber tremble.

'Stop it!' she yelled.

But Dan's voice just rose even louder. Lucy looked around desperately. She had to stop him!

Every inch of Lucy's body began to tingle. She felt as if her skin was glowing. Above her Regulus shone down. As she stared at it, she could feel the magic within her start to grow and swell, start to reach out and try to connect with the stardust in the skies. *Power*, she thought, welcoming it and drawing it up. *My power!*

The air around her fizzed even more. A golden spark shot into the sky.

Dan glanced round, his expression uneasy.

More golden sparks began shooting off Lucy's skin.

Dan stared at her. 'What's happening? You're fighting my magic. But how *can* you . . .?'

With a gasp, Lucy felt power explode from deep down inside her and suddenly her arms were free. Dan's magic bonds were broken. She saw her chance and, without stopping to think, grabbed it. 'Fire be with me!' she yelled. A fireball shot through the air straight at him.

He shouted in shock but flicked his wrist to one side and the fireball bounced away from him as if it had struck an invisible shield. 'How did you break free?' he exclaimed. 'You're just a child! You can't have so much power inside you!'

'Well, I have!' Lucy shouted. She turned to fly but as she took off, a gust of wind sent her sprawling to the ground. She gasped as she thudded down. She had forgotten that dark spirits could control all the elements, not just one!

'You will not escape!' Dan began to mutter some more magic words under his breath.

Lucy felt the invisible ropes tightening around her again. 'No!' she gasped, and she shot a crackling ball of fire shot straight at Dan. He doused it in water. 'Bind her!' he snapped. The bonds tightened again.

Giddiness swept over Lucy. *Give in, give in*, a voice in her head seemed to be saying.

No! A small part of her fought on. But her magic seemed to be fading away to somewhere deep inside her that she couldn't reach. To her horror, she found herself walking into the circle.

Got to stop him, she thought through gritted teeth, the dizziness and sickness coming in waves.

Dan turned to the skies. 'Begin!' he declared, and looking up at the skies he shouted out a string of cruel-sounding words.

Thunder clapped out overhead.

Lucy gasped as she felt power surge across the sky. The stars seemed to glow brighter. 'No!' she exclaimed.

'It has started!' Dan said triumphantly. 'It has begun!'

Lucy had never felt more terrified in her life. The stardust ritual had started. There was no stopping it now!

CHAPTER

Nine

'Lucy!' Hearing four people yelling her name, Lucy looked round. Allegra, Tess, Lottie and Bea were racing towards the stones.

'What are you doing?' Allegra yelled at Dan. 'Leave Lucy alone!' She sent a fierce gust of wind shooting straight at him. He looked startled. But within seconds he had sent two fireballs shooting straight at the four girls.

'Shield be with me!' Tess yelled. A magical shield appeared in front of the girls and the fireballs bounced away.

Taking advantage of Dan's confusion, Allegra sent an even stronger bolt of wind flying straight at him. It hit him in the chest, sending him sprawling backwards. As he began to fall, Lottie and Bea both gasped out, 'Plants! Grow anew!'

Bramble bushes pushed out of the earth. Dan fell into them, the branches tangled in his cloak, the thorns biting into the material. As he struggled, his head hit a stone. Suddenly he lay still.

'He's knocked out!' Lottie cried.

Lucy felt the bonds lift. She shot into the air out of the circle towards the others. 'I'm free!'

'What's been going on?' Tess demanded.

'It's Dan!' Lucy gasped. 'He's a dark spirit!'

'Dan!' Allegra exclaimed, looking round to where the hideous figure was lying in the brambles.

'Yes, he just made himself look young. He really looks like that!' Lucy looked round at them all. 'What are you doing here?'

'I got back and felt really bad that I'd let you come here alone,' said Tess, looking shamefaced. 'I didn't want to tell the grown-ups in case you got into trouble so I told the others . . .'

'And we decided to come and see if you were OK,' Lottie said. 'What was happening? What was he trying to do?'

'The stardust ritual,' Lucy replied.

The others looked horrified.

'No!' whispered Allegra.

Lucy nodded. 'He wanted to use me to draw down power from the skies.' As she spoke there was a loud crackle. She looked up. Magic was gathering in the skies above them. The stars seemed to be glowing more brightly than she had ever seen.

'Quick!' Tess exclaimed. 'Let's get to the cove and tell everyone!'

But a horrible realization was sinking through Lucy. 'No,' she whispered.

'What do you mean, no?' Allegra exclaimed, grabbing her arm. 'Come on, Luce!'

'I can't!' Lucy said. She looked up at the sky. She could sense the magic there. It was getting stronger and stronger every second. 'The ritual's been started and now it can't be stopped. The power in the skies is going to hit the circle. And if there's no one there to take the magic, Dan said it'll strike the earth and kill

everything in the area with its power.
It has to flow into someone or
everything round here will be
destroyed.'

'What are we going to do?' Allegra
cried.

'Maybe we've got time to get back
and get the adults before it happens,'
Tess said.

'But what can they do?' Lucy said
helplessly.

'Nothing!' They swung round. Dan
had stood up. His cloak was ripped and
he had brambles hanging from him. He
faced them from the other side of the
circle, his arms raised. 'You *will* do this,'
he said to Lucy.

'No!' Allegra shouted furiously, diving
towards him. 'You can't have her!'

He hissed a word and Allegra
stopped in the air, unable to move,
caught by his magic.

Before the others could react, Dan
had turned on them and thrown his arm
towards Lottie and Bea. 'Bind them!'

They cried out as their arms were
clamped to their bodies. Lucy knew he
must be using the same magic he'd
used on her back in the circle.

Lucy was horrified but she knew she
didn't have time to help them; she and
Tess had to defend themselves, or they
would all be caught in his magic. At
the same instant she turned to Tess,
Tess turned to her. From the look in
her eyes, Lucy could see that the other
girl had had the same thought.
Without a moment's hesitation they

grabbed hands. 'Shield be with me!' they both yelled the same instant as Dan threw out his hand and yelled, 'Bind them!'

The air around Lucy and Tess shimmered in a silvery, almost see-through circle. As Dan's magic hit the magical barrier, sparks flew into the air but the barrier held fast. Lucy and Tess gripped each other's fingers. Power moved through them, down their hands, and through their fingers, into each other.

More power, more, Lucy thought to herself.

Dan shot out his arm again. 'Bind them!' he shrieked. But although the magical barrier crackled and sparked it held firm.

We've got to do something.

Lucy's eyes flew to Tess's face. The
words hadn't been her own.

Yes, she thought back. Tess gave the
slightest nod.

Lucy couldn't believe it. They were
reading each other's thoughts!

Surprise him. Attack him. Tess's voice came into Lucy's mind.

Dan started moving towards them. He was careful to walk round the circle as he crossed the burial chamber. 'I will break your magic down,' he hissed.

Shield and Fire, Lucy thought.

Yes.

At the exact same moment, just as Dan reached their side of the circle, they let go of each other's hands and swung round.

'Shield be with me!' Tess shouted, pointing her arm just in front of where Dan was about to step.

He gave a surprised gasp as a shield sprang up in front of him.

'Shield be gone!' Tess cried immediately as Lucy shot her arm out.

'Fire be with me!' she yelled.

Lucy shot a burning fire bolt straight at Dan. Suddenly everything seemed to happen at once. Dan was too close to the fire and too surprised to react with magic. He ducked to avoid it, stumbling backwards into the circle. As he lost his concentration, Allegra, Lottie and Bea broke free.

The air seemed to crackle with magic.

Lucy looked up. 'The power!' she gasped.

There was a loud thunderclap. Dan looked up, a horrified expression on his face. The next instant, lightning forked down through the sky. Only this wasn't ordinary lightning – it was lightning made out of stardust, bright white and dazzling. As it hit Dan, his body glowed as the power surged into it.

No! Lucy thought in horror. *It will kill him!*

She hesitated for a second but no matter how dark a spirit he was, and despite what he had been trying to do to her, she couldn't stand by and watch him die.

Suddenly she knew what she must do . . .

Ten

'Hold hands!' she yelled at the others.
'Make a chain! Use the magic! We
have to let it flow back out!'

Dan was standing in the middle
of the circle. His body was rooted to
the ground. He couldn't move or
speak or do anything. The magic was
too strong. Lucy dived into the circle
and grabbed his hand. Her body

jolted as power surged into her.

Magic beat through her body, stronger than she had ever felt before. She could hardly move with the force of it but as Tess's fingers closed around hers she felt the pressure ease slightly as the magic flowed onwards into Tess instead of just building up inside her. She turned her head. Allegra was now holding Tess's other hand, then there was Lottie, and finally Bea who completed the chain.

'Use the magic, Bea!' Lucy gasped as she saw the scared look on Bea's face.

'Grow anew!' Bea shouted. And with her free hand she pointed at the bare soil. Magic crackled through them, pulled down from the stars, into Dan and then through the girls until it exploded out of Bea's fingertips. Plants began to spring up through the ground. Short green grass, spikes of heather, soft thrift, white and red champion . . .

As the magic flowed more and more plants grew until every inch of the bare soil was covered.

'What now?' Bea cried.

Lucy felt Dan move. She turned to look at him. The shock had left his face. He looked up at the sky. 'Finish!' he gasped.

There was a loud crackle and the magic stopped. A grating, creaking noise rang through the air as one of the left-hand stones tipped back slightly like a chair being tilted on its back legs. Lucy gasped, half expecting the whole stone structure to crash down around them but the stone stopped moving and Carywn's Rest held fast.

Lucy drew in a deep, trembling breath. 'Is everyone OK?' she asked.

The others nodded shakily.

'I thought everything was going to fall down on top of us,' Lottie said.

'Look at the earth,' Allegra breathed, staring at the greenery.

'I did it!' Bea whispered, looking round in astonishment. 'I grew all those plants where nothing could grow.'

Lottie hugged her. 'You did! Doesn't it look brilliant?'

'And doesn't the whole place feel so different?' Allegra said. 'Clearer somehow.'

'The bad magic's finally gone,' Tess said in delight.

Lucy looked at Dan. He had
slumped forward on to his knees. 'You
saved me,' he whispered.

'Yes,' Lucy said coldly.

'Why?' he asked.

'Because Lucy's good,' Allegra said,
stepping forward and answering for
her. 'She couldn't let you die.'

Dan stared intently at Lucy. 'You are

the last of the summer spirits. Of course. I see it now.'

Turning, he grabbed something from the hole that had appeared under the standing stone. It looked like a very old book. Before Lucy could do anything, Dan had flown into the air, his body was shaking, his face was pale and haggard.

'Our paths will cross again, Lucy! *Camouflagus!*' he hissed and then he vanished.

'No!' Lucy gasped.

'He's gone!' Allegra exclaimed.

Just then three adults stardust spirits came flying into sight. It was Fran, David and Xanthe.

'Lucy? Allegra? What's been happening?' Xanthe demanded, looking

more anxious than Lucy had ever
seen her.

Lucy looked at the others. They
seemed just as shocked about Dan's
escape as she was. 'It . . . it's a long
story,' she stammered.

The adults landed on the grass. 'Tell
us,' Fran urged. 'We're listening.'

It took quite a while to explain
everything that had happened. At the
end, the adults hugged Lucy and the
others. 'You're so lucky to be OK,'
Fran said.

'It was a fantastic idea to use the
magic for good,' David said, looking at
Lucy with respect. 'By releasing the
power you have cleansed this place,
made it full of good energy again.'

'I'm just glad you're all safe,' Xanthe exclaimed, pulling Lucy and Allegra close.

'What about Dan?' Lucy said. 'He got away.'

'It doesn't matter. The important thing is that you're all safe and that you stopped him completing the ritual.'

'But what if he comes back?'

'He won't,' Xanthe said, looking at the chamber. 'This place has lost its dark energy. He, and other dark spirits like him, won't come here again.'

'Let's go back to the cove and tell the others what's been happening,' Fran said.

'And get ready for the trip to Guillemot Island,' David said. 'I think you could all do with some fun after what you've been through tonight.'

'Actually,' Lucy said quickly as everyone rose into the air. 'I think Tess and I have got something to do first.' She glanced at Tess.

A look of understanding crossed Tess's face. 'It'll only take a few minutes and then we'll catch you up.'

'It's nothing dangerous, is it?' Xanthe asked.

'No,' Lucy replied. 'I promise.'

'OK,' Xanthe replied. See you back at the cove soon. But don't be long.'

Allegra swooped up to Lucy. 'Is it the gorse?'

Lucy nodded.

Allegra grinned. 'See you later then.' And she flew off with the others leaving Lucy and Tess alone.

There was a moment's silence and

then Tess sighed. 'I'm sorry I didn't believe you when you said there was something bad going on here,' she said. 'I shouldn't have let you come on your own.' She looked directly at Lucy. 'I really am sorry.'

'It's OK,' Lucy replied, appreciating the apology. 'I shouldn't really have come here when we'd been told not to. Thanks for telling the others and coming to find me. And for not getting me into trouble by telling the adults.'

Tess lifted her chin. 'I never tell tales.'

'Me neither,' Lucy said.

Their eyes met.

'Oh, I'm sorry I've been mean, Lucy!' The words burst out of Tess. 'I guess I've just been jealous. Mum and Dad made such a big thing about you coming. They just kept talking about how powerful you were and how you could do all sorts of amazing things.'

Lucy smiled at her. 'I'm not surprised you hated me then. I think *I* would have done if I was you!' She shook her head. 'Let's forget it.'

'Thanks.' Tess hesitated. 'You know . . .' She sounded almost embarrassed for once. '. . . Lottie and Bea have been going on about how we are quite alike.'

Lucy stared. 'Allegra thinks that too.'

'I didn't think so but I'm not so sure now. Doing that magic together was so cool,' Tess said. 'It was like we could read each other's thoughts.'

'Yeah,' Lucy grinned. 'Do you want to go and do some more?'

'Yes. Let's!' Tess said.

They flew to the area of gorse they had been trying to clear. Working together, they finished off the task in hardly any time at all. As the last gorse bush burnt to the ground, leaving the soil now clear to regenerate and grow new plants, Lucy and Tess exchanged high fives.

'I feel better now!' Lucy said.

'Me too!' Tess said. 'Let's go and find the others!'

When Lucy and Tess got back to the cove, they found everyone getting ready to go to Guillemot Island. It was quite a long flight but it was worth it. As they approached, Lucy saw that there were birds nesting on every ledge of the cliffs – puffins, auks and kittiwakes.

She swooped up to explore with
the others. The land was covered with
a sea of spring flowers. Sheep grazed
the land and as the girls flew over
they could see lambs lying beside
their mothers. They even spotted a
herd of deer and a small group of
wild ponies.

After a while, Tess led the way to a
sloping cliff. 'This is a good place to
sit and watch the sun come up,' she
said, as they sat down on the short
grass. On the craggy rocks below
ten fat grey seals were snoozing.

'I like the seal pups,' Tess said.
'They're so cute – all white and
fluffy. You'll have to come back in
the autumn when they're all being

born,' she said to Lucy and Allegra.

'Yes, please!' Lucy said. She and Tess smiled at each other.

'I'm going to miss you when you go home,' Bea said to Lucy and Allegra. 'I've done more powerful magic since you've been here than I've ever done in my life. It's been great.'

'You'll have to keep practising and show us what you can do next time we come,' Lucy said. Just then Xanthe walked past, and she jumped to her feet. 'I'll be back in a minute.'

'Hi, Lucy. Are you OK?' Xanthe asked as Lucy ran up.

Lucy nodded. 'Xanthe, can I ask you something?' She checked that she was out of earshot of the others. There was something she had to know.

'Of course,' Xanthe said curiously. 'What is it?'

Lucy paused. 'Dan said something weird to me. He called me the last of the summer spirits.'

Xanthe looked at her, but said nothing.

'What did he mean?' Lucy asked.

Xanthe hesitated and then shook her head. 'It's just an old saying, Lucy. It doesn't mean anything that important. Don't worry about it.'

'But . . .' Lucy began.

'Hush now,' Xanthe said, touching her hair. 'You've had enough to think about today already.' She pointed into the distance where the dark sky was just starting to lighten. 'The sun will be rising soon. We must fly

home before the stars vanish and our
magic wears off.' She looked round.
'Your friends are waiting for you.'

Lucy could tell the subject was
closed. 'OK,' she sighed. She made her
way back to her friends.

'Hey! Look!' Allegra exclaimed,
pointing to the sea as Lucy rejoined
them. 'Dolphins!'

Lucy gasped. Allegra was right. A
group of dolphins had swum into
the bay.

'Come on! Let's go and fly with
them as they swim!' Tess exclaimed
eagerly.

She dived through the air
towards the sea. The others followed
her. The dolphins saw them coming
and stuck their heads out of the waves,

opening their mouths in friendly grins.

'Oh, wow!' Lucy breathed, looking at the beautiful creatures with their grey skin and bright dark eyes. Two of them leapt out of the water below her and dived back into the waves. Water splashed up. Lucy whizzed out of the way just in time.

'Let's fly with them!' Tess cried as the group of dolphins set off across the sea, leaping and jumping.

Tess, Allegra, Lottie and Bea raced after the dolphins, giggling as they dodged the spray.

Lucy felt her troubles slip away. And, with a laugh of delight, she swooped after the others just as the first rays of the sun streaked across the dark sky.

Do you love magic, unicorns and fairies?

Join the sparkling

Linda Chapman

fan club today!

It's FREE!

You will receive
an exciting **online newsletter** 4 times a year,
packed full of fun, games, news and competitions.

How to join:
visit
lindachapman.co.uk
and enter your details

or send your name, address, date of birth* and email address to:

linda.chapman@puffin.co.uk